Because of Thursday

Because of Thursday

PATRICIA POLACCO

A PAULA WISEMAN BOOK
SIMON & SCHUSTER BOOKS FOR YOUNG READERS
NEW YORK LONDON TORONTO SYDNEY NEW DELHI

Thursdays had always been lucky for Annie Fetlock.

She was born on a Thursday.

She won her first cooking contest at the age of eight on a Thursday.

She met the love of her life, Mario, on a Thursday.

They were married on a bright Thursday afternoon, and their two children were each born on a Thursday. One in June and the other in July.

It was actually on a Thursday that Annie and Mario opened their diner together. And it was on a Thursday that Annie made her signature creation. A splendid pasta salad.

People came from far and wide just to taste it. After one bite they devoured it, almost in a single gulp, then wanted more! Annie called it Poke Salad, because the more you poked at it, the more scrumptious, succulent, delectable surprises you'd find hidden in, under, and around the pasta. As a matter of fact, everyone called Annie . . . Poke Salad Annie!

As the years passed, Poke Salad became an institution in that little town. People came from other towns, then other cities, then other states, and even other countries. It was almost as if Poke Salad cast a spell on anyone who ate it so they'd just keep coming back over and over again!

Mario, Annie, and the boys were happy as Harry to be part of that little diner. Eventually, just as Annie and Mario had planned, both boys went off to fancy colleges and graduated with honors. They both became big-time lawyers, and as much as they truly loved Annie and Mario, they had to move away to big cities to practice law. But Annie and Mario got wonderful letters from them every other Thursday. Just like clockwork. And the boys came home for visits regular-like. Whenever they were in town, they always loved helping out at the diner!

One day Mario complained that he wasn't feeling so well. It was a Tuesday. After a time he couldn't quite come to the diner like he used to.

It was a Friday when the doctors gave Mario and Annie real bad news.

It was on a Monday that Annie's beloved Mario passed away.

Annie was inconsolable! Her heart just wasn't in that little diner anymore. It seemed that all the joy and mirth that made that place . . . was gone!

Pretty soon there were fewer and fewer surprises in her Poke Salad. After a time folks just stopped coming in. Her broken heart seemed to make her food sad.

Annie finally closed the place.

Well, sir, without that diner that little old town pretty much dried up. Most days Annie took to her porch and sat in her rocker and stared off into space.

That is, until one day she heard the tiniest little sound coming from a dish towel that was all rolled up and stuffed behind the butter churn on the edge of her porch.

When Annie went to pick it up, she noticed that whoever had left it there had hand embroidered the word "Thursday" on it.

"Well, I'll be. . . . TODAY IS THURSDAY!" Annie whispered as she peeled back the folds of the dish towel.

That's when she saw it.

The most darlin' little kitten she had ever seen.

A little boy kitten!

He was hungry and covered in fleas. His eyes were dirty, and his little nose needed cleaning.

Annie scrubbed him up, warmed milk, and fed it to him with an eyedropper.

Annie was in love! Something about him reminded her of Mario.

She knew if she named him, he was staying with her forever.

"Little feller," she cooed, "I'm calling you Thursday!"

And so it was. . . . Thursday found a home right there with Annie.

She framed that dish towel he came in and hung it right over her TV.

She and Thursday sat and watched all the cooking shows. Their favorite was
the one with the traveling chef who visited small restaurants and diners all over
the country.

One day Annie's two neighbor kids came over for a visit. They fell in love with Thursday too and started coming over almost every single day just to play with him. They even taught him amazing tricks. Turned out he could jump and balance on anything!

"Long as you two are here, I might as well fix you something to eat!" Annie crowed one day. And for the first time in ages she got out all of her pots and pans and commenced cooking.

"Let's see . . . three parts joy . . . four parts giggles, and a pinch of mirth and a couple of mule kicks and a ton of love," she sang out as she spooned a pasta delight on the plates of her young guests.

She cooked for those kids almost every day and then sent food home with them for their families.

One day the kitchen was filled with delicious clouds of steaming, bubbling wonder. The pots made ringing sounds as they danced on the stove, and something irresistible was wafting from the oven.

"What's cookin', Miss Annie?" Jake the mailman asked as he stuck his head through the kitchen door.

"I'm making something that I haven't made in a very, very long time," Annie sang out.

"Is it your Poke Salad, Annie?" Jake chirped as he eased himself into one of the kitchen chairs.

About then Jim the fireman pushed his head into the kitchen door.
"You makin' what I think you're a-makin'?" he inquired as he took a seat.
"Come on in, Jimmie . . . I'll plate some up for you!"

"Hot dog, Miss Annie . . . POKE SALAD!" he trumpeted as he dove
into his bowl of pasta.

After that, almost every noon as regular as clockwork Annie started
feeding not only Jake, Jim, and the kids, but Harley the insurance man,
who told Lester Johnson, who told Betty Swindon, and pretty soon just
about every one of Miss Annie's regulars showed up. Not only did her
guests enjoy their Poke Salad, but the children had Thursday do some of
his spectacular tricks to entertain them.

Didn't take long for Annie to realize that there just wasn't room in her
kitchen for any more guests. So she decided to open the diner again.

Of course it was a Thursday!

Almost all of the townsfolk helped Annie scrub and clean that old diner.

Pretty soon it was shipshape and ready for business.

The ribbon-cutting ceremony was on a Thursday!

"I'm reopening this here diner 'cause so many folks need feedin'!" Annie announced as everyone cheered.

Of course Thursday the cat was a constant presence at the diner. Mr. Briggs of the county health department probably should have objected, but he'd missed Annie's Poke Salad so much he wasn't about to tell her that Thursday couldn't be there. Besides, her customers loved watching that little cat do his dazzling array of tricks.

Well, let me tell you. Almost as soon as that little joint opened up, the word got out. People were flocking there from just about everywhere.

"Poke Salad Annie Is Back," the headlines read. Annie's diner had put her little town on the map again.

Then one day a low, lean, red convertible car growled down Main Street and pulled up right in front of Annie's diner.

A mysterious figure sneaked out of the car and slithered into the diner, trying very hard not to be seen. Luckily, the place was jumping, so he managed to take a seat in the farthest corner without being noticed.

In the kitchen things were busy, busy, busy. Annie had a huge pot of drained pasta about to be made into Poke Salad. Chef Rotund, her helper, had another saucepan full of olive oil and garlic. Thursday started doing his tricks.

Thursday jumped, leaped, and twisted in midair, always landing just right while the customers gasped. But today the kitty miscalculated and overjumped. He glanced off the bowl of draining rigatoni, which made the cans of garlic and red pepper flakes spill into the pasta. Then the entire container of parmesan cheese overturned into the oil, garlic, pepper flakes, and pasta. . . . The grated cheese covered all of the pasta, making it an oily, garlicky mess!

Then all of the kitchen help stopped and peered into the pot of garlic goo.

"That there is the ugliest pasta I've ever seen!" Chef Rotund wheezed.

He was quite right, you know. It looked like it had been kicked around in the dirt with all the burned pepper flakes in it and wiped through someone's armpit with all the lumps of garlic on it and blown across a dusty field with all the grated cheese on it.

If that wasn't ugly enough, the dark olive oil looked like it had come out of the crankcase of an old jalopy!

But here's the thing: IT HAD THE MOST AMAZING AROMA!

As everyone in the diner breathed in the delectable fragrance, the mystery man in the corner could no longer resist. He leaped from his seat, grabbed a fork, and took a running start and dove into the mountain of gelatinous garlic glop, stabbed it, and shoved it into his mouth!

"SHUT THE FRONT DOOR!" he sang out. "This is OUTSTANDING . . . OFF THE HOOK . . . OUTSIDE THE BOX . . . OUT OF BOUNDS! I'M ON THE FAST TRAIN TO FLAVORTOWN!" he roared as he took handfuls of the pasta and threw it into his mouth. "THIS IS THE MONEY!"

Annie couldn't believe her eyes. It was that famous TV chef who visits diners!

"THIS STUFF IS RIGHTEOUS!" he gurgled as he spun around the counter.

That's when all of the customers started stampeding.

With a collective leap they jostled for positions to sample the Ugly Pasta.

Then absolutely everyone groaned with joy, pleasure, and ecstasy.

They all agreed that they had never tasted pasta like that in their entire lives!

"I'm telling you, Annie . . . THIS STUFF IS RIDICULOUSLY FLAVORFUL . . . OFF THE HOOK . . . AMAZING . . . AND NEEDS TO BE OUT THERE!" the traveling chef exclaimed.

"You need to open pasta parlors all over the country that serve this stuff," he added as he leaped into his car. "I'll be back with a film crew. . . . We need to put you and this place on national television!" he called out as he sped away.

Yes, sir . . . Annie, with the help of her wondrous performing kitty, had stumbled onto another discovery that would change culinary history! They had discovered UGLY PASTA, and . . . of course . . . it was Thursday!

Sure enough, after the diner was featured on TV, Ugly Pasta became a household name. And with the help of her two sons, the Ugly Pasta Diners became a national franchise. Annie knew just what to do with the profits that were rolling in. First she opened a pasta and sauce manufacturing plant on the edge of her village. Everyone in her town who had been out of work now had a job! Then she opened a mega youth center. Finally she formed a foundation that granted numerous scholarships for deserving young people so they could attend college.

Now, one would expect Annie to retire and live in a luxury mansion in a warm climate. But Annie loved her little farmhouse and stayed put. The true joy of her life was to rise each morning, trundle to the village with Thursday, and open her little diner. Nothing made her happier than making Poke Salad and Ugly Pasta and serving it to her customers while they watched Thursday perform. Occasionally Annie would sigh and whisper, "To think that all that has happened is because of this little cat . . . all because of Thursday!"

There are many recipes for Ugly Pasta. Though its name can be off-putting, its taste is unforgettable. Every cook makes the recipe his or her own. You'll have to come by my house to taste my recipe. Here is a basic recipe to get you started:

Ugly Pasta à la Patricia Polacco

This is a recipe to make with a trusted adult. Not to be made without adult supervision. I hesitated to put this in a children's book. The hot oil is dangerous. Be careful!

INGREDIENTS

- 2 cups (16 ounces) good quality olive oil
- 1 cup dried red pepper flakes
- Six 4-ounce jars minced garlic, drained, or 4 cups chopped garlic
- 1 pound pasta, any shape
- salt, to taste
- Four 16-ounce jars Parmesan cheese

DIRECTIONS

Pour the olive oil into a saucepan. Bring to a boil. When oil is hot enough to smoke, carefully add the dried red pepper flakes and garlic to the olive oil. Be careful. The oil is very hot. It will almost explode. Not for children to try.

Simmer the garlic and red pepper flakes until the garlic is golden brown.

In a separate pot, cook the pasta, al dente, in salted water. Drain the pasta, return to its pot, then pour the hot oil, garlic, and pepper mixture over the pasta. Stir and toss until oil, garlic, and pepper evenly coats the pasta. Then toss in the Parmesan cheese. Stir well.

Eat warm, not hot. And it is actually best when it has sat for a time.

Patricia Polacco at home with her cat,
Thursday, who inspired this story.

For my friends at Ole's Diner in Alameda, California, and
to darlin' Thursday

This book is a work of fiction. Any references to historical events, real people, or real places
are used fictitiously. Other names, characters, places, and events are products
of the author's imagination, and any resemblance to actual events or places or persons,
living or dead, is entirely coincidental.

SIMON & SCHUSTER BOOKS FOR YOUNG READERS
An imprint of Simon & Schuster Children's Publishing Division
1230 Avenue of the Americas, New York, New York 10020
Copyright © 2016 by Patricia Polacco
All rights reserved, including the right of reproduction in whole or in part in any form.
SIMON & SCHUSTER BOOKS FOR YOUNG READERS is a trademark of Simon & Schuster, Inc.
For information about special discounts for bulk purchases, please contact Simon & Schuster Special Sales
at 1-866-506-1949 or business@simonandschuster.com.
The Simon & Schuster Speakers Bureau can bring authors to your live event.
For more information or to book an event, contact the Simon & Schuster Speakers Bureau
at 1-866-248-3049 or visit our website at www.simonspeakers.com.
Book design by Laurent Linn
The text for this book was set in Warnock Pro.
The illustrations for this book were rendered in two and six B pencils and acetone markers.
Manufactured in China
0816 SCP
First Edition
2 4 6 8 10 9 7 5 3 1
Library of Congress Cataloging-in-Publication Data
Polacco, Patricia, author, illustrator.
Because of Thursday / Patricia Polacco. — First edition.
pages cm
"A Paula Wiseman book."
Summary: "Annie Fetlock—born on Thursday, met the love of her life on Thursday,
and when a special cat comes into her life on Thursday, she knows he has found
the right home"— Provided by publisher.
ISBN 978-1-4814-2140-9 (hardcover) — ISBN 978-1-4814-2143-0 (ebook)
[1. Days—Fiction. 2. Cats—Fiction.] I. Title.
PZ7.P75186Bd 2016
[E]—dc23
2014019154